For Shale and Ever. When something
extraordinary shows up in your life,
I hope you see it for what it is… a gift.

~Dad

Thanks to my friends
for always supporting me.

~Mae Besom

WHAT DO YOU DO WITH A CHANCE?

Written by Kobi Yamada ⧗ Illustrated by Mae Besom

One day, I got a chance.

It just seemed to show up. It acted like
it knew me, as if it wanted something.

I didn't know why it was here.
"What do you do with a chance?"
I wondered.

It fluttered around me. It brushed up against me. It circled me as if it wanted me to grab it. I started to reach for it, but I was unsure and pulled back.

And so it flew away.

I thought about it a lot. I wished I had taken my chance.
I realized I had wanted it, but I still didn't know if I had the courage.

When another chance came around,
I wasn't so sure. But I decided to try.

I went to reach for it, but I missed and fell.
I was embarrassed. I felt foolish. It seemed like
everyone was looking at me.

I decided I never wanted to feel this way again.

So after that, whenever a chance
came along, I ignored it.

And the more I ignored them,
the less they came around.

Until one day I noticed that I hadn't seen a chance
in quite a while. It was as if they had all disappeared.
I started to worry, "What if I don't get another chance?"

I know I acted like I didn't care, but the truth was,
I did. I still wanted to take a chance, but I was afraid.
And I wasn't sure if I would ever be brave enough.

Then I thought, "Maybe I don't have to be brave *all the time*. Maybe I just need to be brave for a little while at *the right time*."

I realized it was up to me.

I promised myself that if I ever got another chance, I wasn't going to hold back. If I got another chance, I was going to be ready.

Then, one seemingly ordinary day,
I saw something shining far off in the distance.

"Is it possible?" I hoped. "Could this be my chance?"

I had to find out. I ran as hard
and as fast as I could toward it.

I don't know how to explain it,
but the second I let go of my fears,
I was full of excitement.

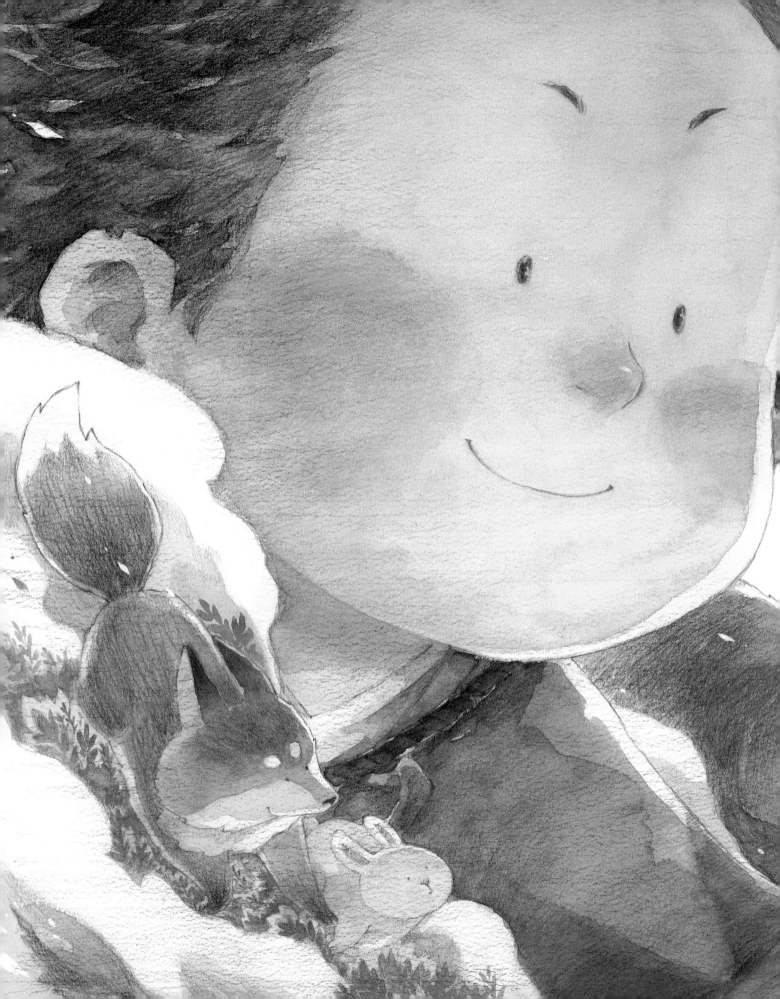

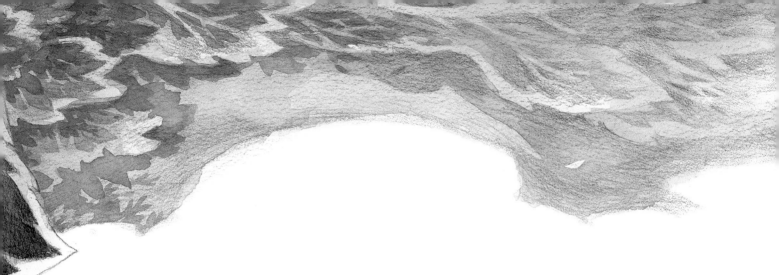

It wasn't that I was no longer afraid, but now my excitement was bigger than my fear.

As I got closer, I could see that this was a really huge chance!

But this time I was ready. As it came by, I reached
out and grabbed it. I held on with all my might.

It felt so good to soar, to fly, to be free!

I now see that when I hold back, I miss out.
And I don't want to miss out. There's just
so much I want to see and do and discover.

So, what do you do with a chance?

You take it… because it just might be
the start of something incredible.

WITH SPECIAL THANKS TO THE ENTIRE COMPENDIUM FAMILY.

CREDITS:

Written by: Kobi Yamada

Illustrated by: Mae Besom

Edited by: Amelia Riedler

Design & Art Direction by: Sarah Forster

Library of Congress Control Number: 2017943400

ISBN: 978-1-943200-73-3

1st printing. Printed in China with soy inks. A011710001